1. Mothers fiction

Dear Parents:

The **Ready Reader Storybooks**™ were created especially for
children in kindergarten through second grade. This series
is designed to increase children's reading skills and promote
their interest in reading by themselves. The stories are
enjoyable, with easy-to-follow plot structures and familiar
settings. Colorful illustrations help develop young
imaginations while adding visual appeal to the reading
experience. Young children will be comfortable with the
format and the large type.

With a variety of stories to accommodate individual interests,
the **Ready Reader Storybooks**™ can help develop basic
abilities and encourage your children's independent reading.

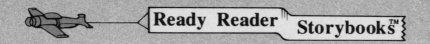
MOM'S DAY OFF

Written by Eugene Bradley Coco
Illustrated by Colette Van Mierlo

MODERN PUBLISHING
A Division of Unisystems, Inc.
New York, New York 10022

Our mom works hard.

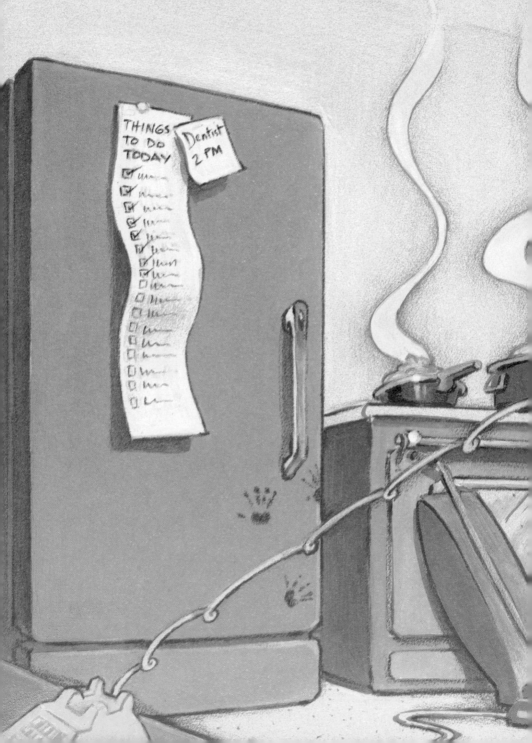

She cooks.

She cleans.

She sews our clothes
when they rip.

She takes care of us
when we're sick.

She even helps with
our homework.

Today mom looks tired.

"Take the day off,"
we tell her.

First we start breakfast.
"Oh no! Watch the
eggs!" I shout.

Mom helps us clean up.

Next we straighten up
the den.

Sally starts to sweep.

There is so much dust.

Mom helps us clear
the dust.

Soon it's time for Ginger's bath.
I turn on the water.

Sally gets Ginger.

The tub is almost full.

"Wait! The faucet is stuck!"

I scream.

Here comes Mom.

The laundry is next.

We put the clothes in
the machine and add soap.
Sally turns the washer on.

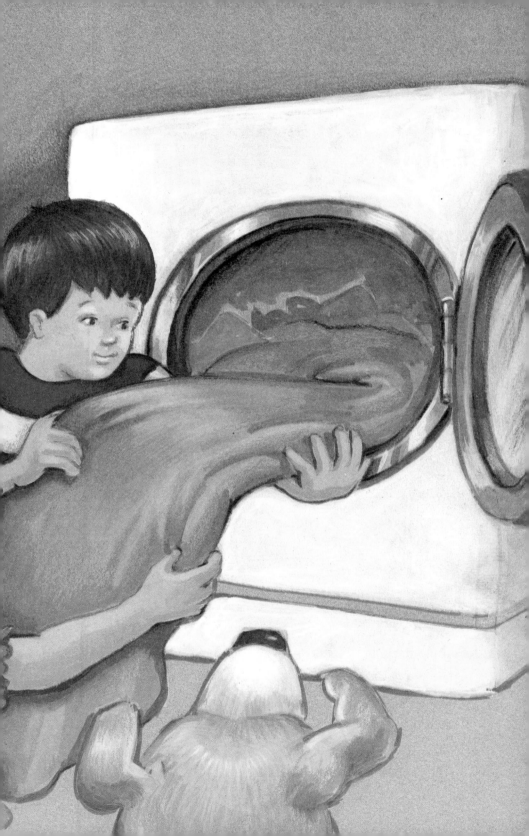

Oops!

The door isn't closed.

"Mom!" we yell.
Mom helps us pick up
the clothes.

Being in charge is hard work.
"Why don't you take
the rest of the day off?"
says Mom.

Thanks, Mom.